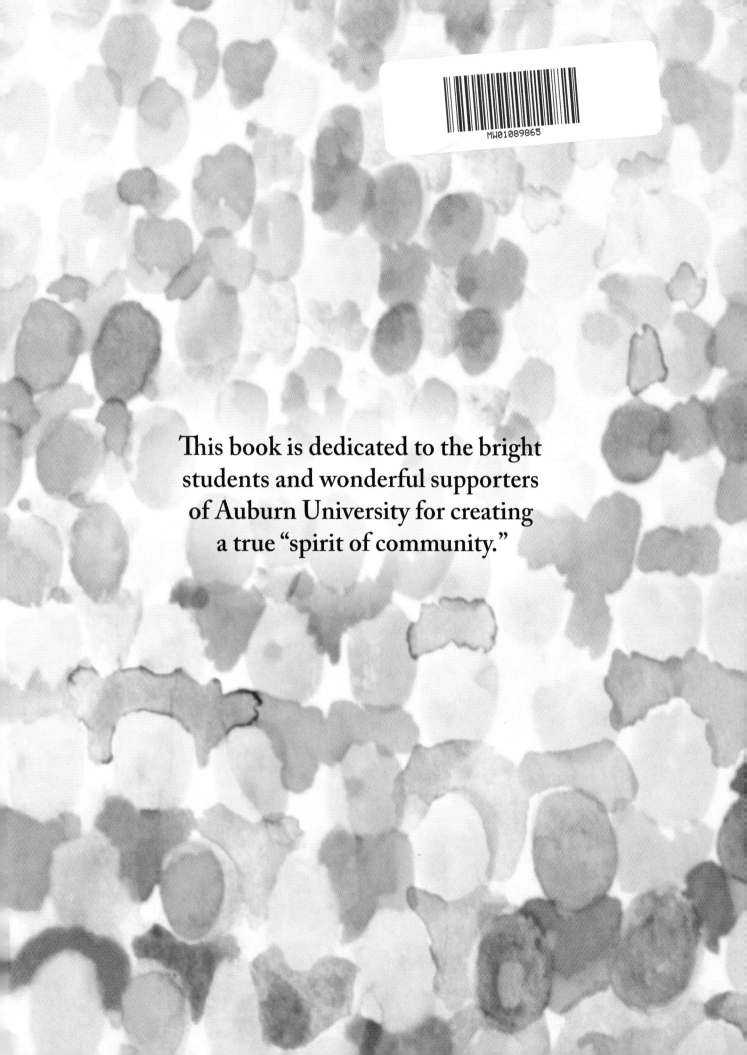

This book is dedicated to the bright students and wonderful supporters of Auburn University for creating a true "spirit of community."

A portion of the proceeds from the sale of this book will go to the
Auburn University Center for Children, Youth, and Families
for outreach and student scholarships.

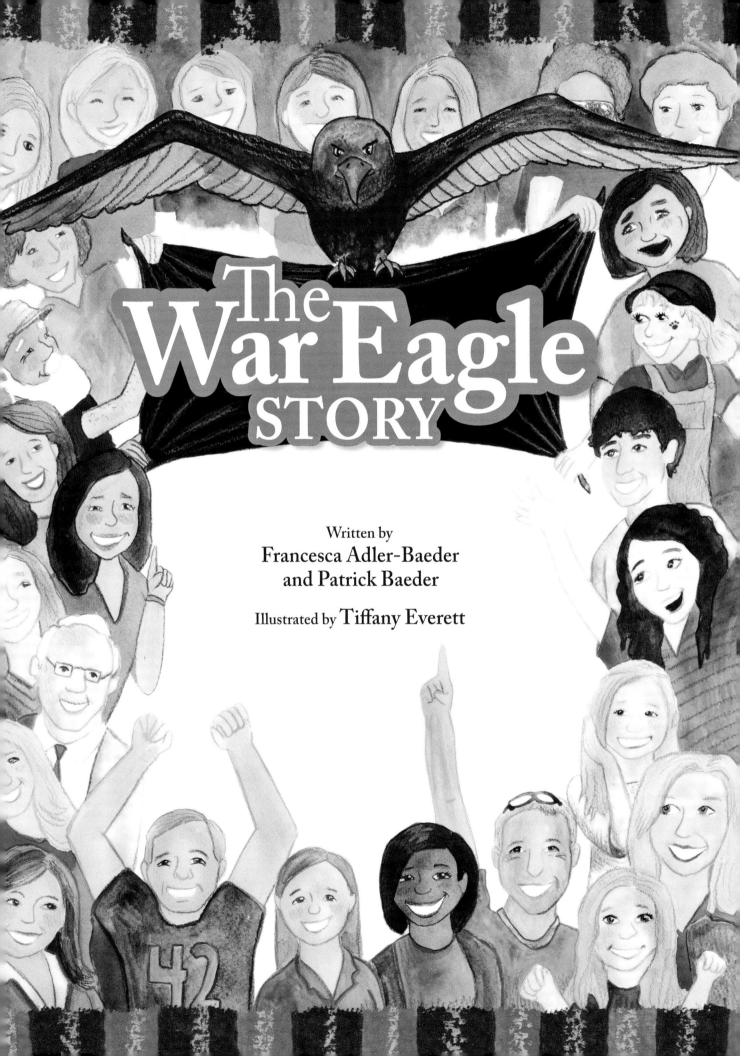

The War Eagle STORY

Written by
**Francesca Adler-Baeder
and Patrick Baeder**

Illustrated by Tiffany Everett

Once upon a time,
A long time ago,
The Auburn Tigers took the field
To face a fearsome foe.

In the stands were the Auburn faithful,
Not just from Alabama.
Some came in suits, some came in skirts,
Some even wore pajamas.

It was not a great day.
The boys were not on their game.
The crowd was not happy;
They were calling their name –

"Come on, Tigers – do something!
By these guys, we can't be beat!
How awful; how embarrassing
To face this defeat!"

In the crowd that day
Sat an old man and his bird.
In the big War of the States he'd fought,
So they'd heard.

He'd found an eagle when young,
In the aftermath of a battle.
The nest was blown from a rock
And hit the ground with a rattle.

He nursed the brave bird
And saw him grow stronger.
But the battles waged on,
Seeming longer and longer.

The man grew more weary
But his bird would soon take wing.
This bird had a mission –
Or some sort of *thing*.

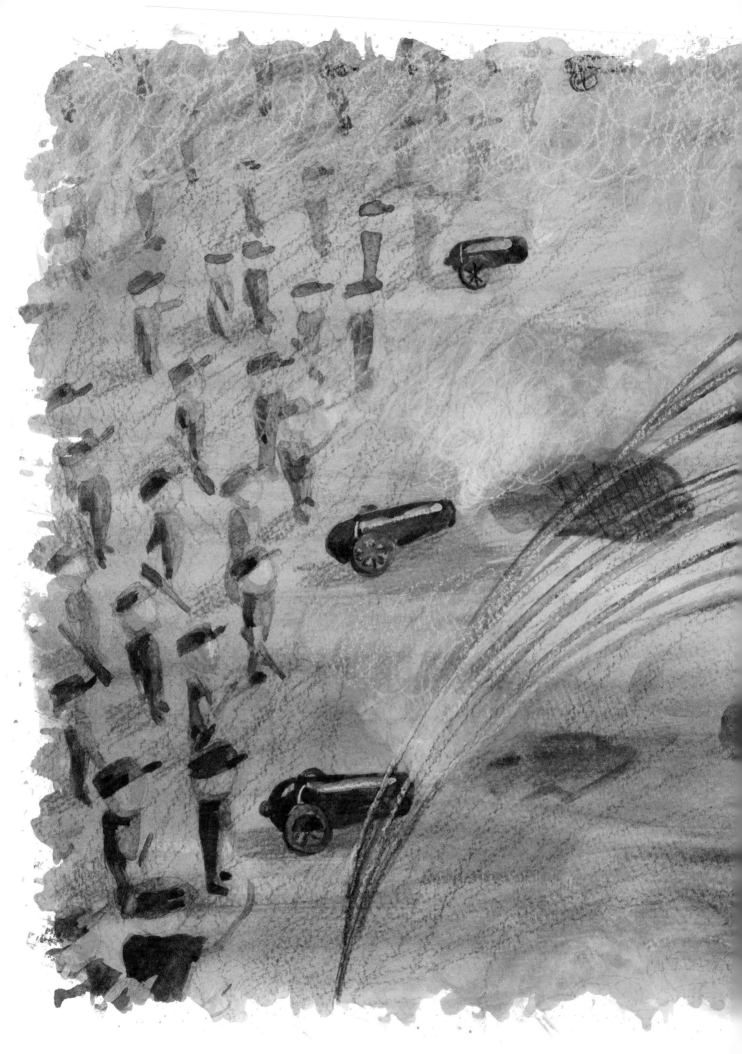

One day all seemed lost
On both sides of the fight.
When upward soared the eagle,
And the men stopped to admire this sight.

What strength! What grace!
What magnificent power!
It filled the soldiers with awe
In their most desperate hour.

This man would live on for many more years,
And now he had grown very old.
His bird on his shoulder sat silently,
No more did he soar so bold.

The soldier sat next to a bright little girl.
He asked her, "What is your name?"
"Aubie Lou," she answered,
Her face turning from the game.

"Where'd you get your bird?"
Asked the girl.
"In the war, my dear; but he's old,
And his wings no longer unfurl."

But all their small talk ended,
And they both grew quiet and sad.
They turned to look upon the field,
The score was so very bad.

They watched their team struggle and fight.
The boys tried, but lost yard after yard.
When suddenly, up from the stands rose the eagle,
Higher and higher he flew...and so far!

He soared! He swooped!
He screeched his eagly sound.
The fans gazed up and wondered,
What in the world had he found?

"That crazy bird!" – called fan one.
"Look out below!" laughed and called fan two.
But she watched him circle and felt the pride,
That little Aubie Lou.

She felt his spirit and strength;
She saw him brave and true.
She looked at the boys on the team,
And knew just what to do….

"Come on, y'all!" she called as she ran...
"I know you can do it –
You're Tiger fans!"

"The spirit – the pride;
You have it, just try!"
Then they all joined in,
With the most *deafening* cry...

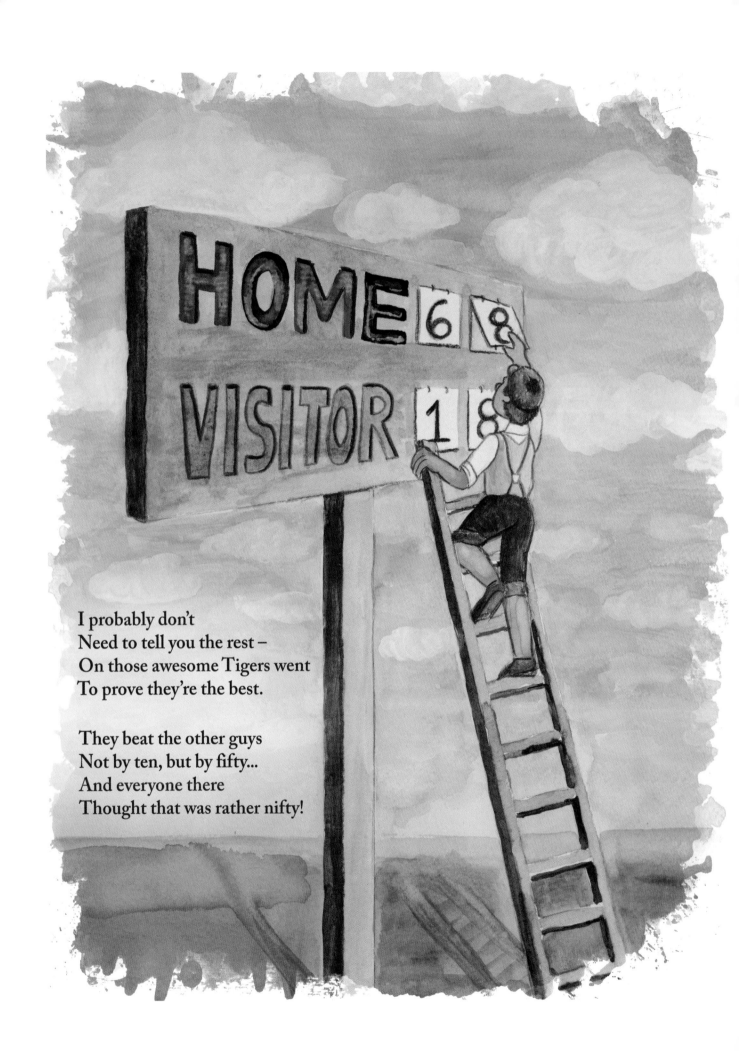

I probably don't
Need to tell you the rest –
On those awesome Tigers went
To prove they're the best.

They beat the other guys
Not by ten, but by fifty...
And everyone there
Thought that was rather nifty!

Well, the regal eagle soared
One final time around.
Then halted mid-air,
And crashed toward the ground.

A gasp went up
From the crowd, from the team
Their War Eagle down –
What could it mean?

Hushed, they watched as the eagle seemed to fade,
Aubie Lou gently lifted him, then shouted,
"It's ok – he just needs some *lemonade*!!"

Once again, he flew skyward
As the spirited cheer arose –

"Waaaaaaaaaaaaar Eagle.........Hey!!!!!

It was on that day,
So many years ago –
An eagle and his loyal friends,
Gave us what we know -

As Auburn Pride;
That winning Tiger spirit –

And, that's our story –
And we're sticking to it!

The End